The Skin on My Chin

By Michelle Chalmers

Author Note

The Skin on My Chin, provides an opportunity to engage in a conversation with children, about skin. Children notice differences in skin color, at a very young age, and sometimes they have questions. Skin is a part of our body we rely on every day, and it's important to understand what it does, but equally as important to learn what skin doesn't or can't do. These conversations are important because stereotypes about skin, and more literally skin color, permeate our society and can send mixed messages to children. It's a great opportunity, while reading this book to your child(ren), to ask questions about how they might already have beliefs about skin, and talk about it. Maybe talk about your own beliefs too, and how you have come to understand how stereotypes hurt everyone.

Please find other possible questions, books and resources beginning on

page 21.

Michelle Chalmers, MSW
Facilitator of Diversity Conversations
www.theskinonmychin.com

Every day I see the skin on my chin.

It's always there when I frown or grin.

It covers my chin and all of my face,

my entire body without missing a space.

Skin comes in many shades
and textures for free...

with freckles or pimples or warts
on my knee.

All the colors of skin we see,

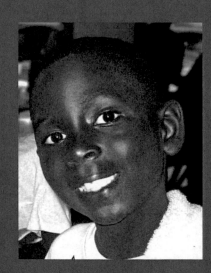

are determined by our family tree.

Skin does have a purpose,
for you and for me,

to cover every bone and artery.

It's hard work to protect
all my insides, I'd say!

And keep me warm
on an icy cold day.

Skin is our armor
that's with us for life.

So, be sure to be careful
with a sharp knife.

Skin is just skin
and works the same way,

no matter who you are,
no matter what day.

It can't make you funny

or fast on your feet,

able to dance or sing to a beat.

Skin doesn't decide if you grow

a little or a lot, strong or weak,

smart or not.

Skin shouldn't have power
to tell me about you.

I must get to know you,
to learn what is true.

There's no other story
          to tell about skin;

it is what it is
          on my chinny chin chin.

Glossary

Stereotype - A set of inaccurate, simplistic generalizations about a group that limits individual uniqueness and allows others to categorize them and treat them accordingly.

http://www.thefreedictionary.com

Melanin - Is a pigment that affects skin, eye, and hair color in humans and other mammals. People whose ancestors lived for long periods in the regions of the globe near the equator generally have larger quantities of melanin in their skins, making their skins dark brown or black and protecting them against high levels of UV exposure. In areas of the globe closer to the poles, people have far less need for protection from ultraviolet, so their skin is usually lighter in color.

http://encyclopedia.kids.net.au/page/me/Melanin

Prejudice - An adverse judgment or opinion formed beforehand or without knowledge or examination of the facts.

http://www.thefreedictionary.com

Questions and Conversations

These questions may be used to begin a conversation after reading this book to your child(ren).

1. **Do you have any questions?** Listen and be careful to answer the question that is asked. Sometimes that might mean asking more questions, to clarify the meaning of what is being asked/said.

2. **What is the purpose of our skin?** This is a great open-ended question to let children talk about what they have learned and noticed about their skin.

3. **Why do people have different shades/colors of skin?** This may be an opportunity to talk about melanin and how our ancestry (family tree) determines the color of our skin, due to where in the world our ancestors originated from.

4. **Has anyone ever learned that the color of skin, could tell you something about a person? If so, what?** This may be an opportunity to talk about the word stereotype.

Questions and Conversations

5. Why can't skin make you funny, fast or smart?

This is a great question to get children thinking. Refer back to pages 16 and 17 to use the pictures, to aid in your discussion. In addition, you may also suggest other things our society gives power to, but has no relevance or scientific truth. Help children to think of things, they have seen or heard, that are believed to have an effect on people's abilities or disabilities, but when truly questioned, isn't possible. For example, if you walk under a ladder or a black cat passes your path. These things may be believed to effect things, but is not based on anything factual. Product marketing also places power on things like shoes or sports drinks that may enhance your athletic abilities, which have no merit.

Having these conversations can sometimes be difficult. Many of us, who have never thought or talked about issues of skin color or race before, may be fearful. It may be scary to not know what to say. However, it is okay if you don't know an answer; let the child know that you are unsure and would like to find out the answer; or find it together and then talk about it. We may also be fearful of saying something wrong. This is a very common feeling. Let the child know you have learned better information and engage in the conversation again; and open the dialogue for your child to ask more questions.

Books

Ada, Alma Flor., and Kathryn Dyble Thompson. *My Name Is María Isabel*.
New York: Aladdin Paperbacks, 1995. Print.

Adoff, Arnold, and Emily Arnold McCully. *Black Is Brown Is Tan*.
New York: Amistad, 2004. Print.

Aldrich, Andrew R., and Mike Motz. *How My Family Came to Be - Daddy, Papa and Me*. Oakland, CA: New Family, 2003. Print.

Atinuke, and Lauren Tobia. *Anna Hibiscus*. Tulsa, OK: Kane Miller, 2010. Print.

Bruchac, Joseph, and S. S. Burrus. *Four Ancestors: Stories, Songs, and Poems from Native North America*. [Mahwah, N.J.]: BridgeWater, 1996. Print.

Czech, Jan M., and Maurie Manning. *The Coffee Can Kid*. Washington, DC: Child & Family, 2002. Print.

Davol, Marguerite W., and Irene Trivas. *Black, White, Just Right*.
Morton Grove, IL: A. Whitman, 1993. Print.

Hamanaka, Sheila. *All the Colors of the Earth*. London: Mantra, 1996. Print.

Hoffman, Mary, and Caroline Binch. *Amazing Grace*. New York: Dial for Young Readers, 1991. Print.

Katz, Karen. *The Colors of Us*. New York: Henry Holt and, 1999. Print.

Kissinger, Katie, and Wernher Krutein. *All the Colors We Are: The Story of How We Get Our Skin Color*. St. Paul, MN: Redleaf, 1994. Print.

Books

Lacapa, Kathleen, and Michael Lacapa. *Less than Half, More than Whole*. Flagstaff, AZ: Northland, 1994. Print.

Mandelbaum, Pili. *You Be Me, I'll Be You*. Brooklyn, NY: Kane/Miller, 1990. Print.

Mochizuki, Ken, Dom Lee, and Yōko Yuri. *Kakoi O Koeta Hōmuran*. Tōkyō: Iwasaki Shoten, 1993. Print.

Ringgold, Faith. *Bonjour, Lonnie*. New York, NY: Hyperion, 1996. Print.

Uchida, Yoshiko, and Joanna Yardley. *The Bracelet*. New York: Philomel, 1993. Print.

Websites

RACE - The Power of An Illusion, **http://www.pbs.org/race**

Becoming Human, **http://www.becominghuman.org**, The Institute of Human Origins, Arizona State University 2001

National Association of School Psychologists, **http://www.nasponline.org/resources/culturalcompetence/diversitywebsites.aspx**

About the Author

This is the first children's book for Michelle Chalmers, MSW who lives in Wellesley, Massachusetts with her husband and two sons.

Please visit:

www.theskinonmychin.com

This book is dedicated to my two beautiful sons, who I love with all my heart.

24118774R00017

Made in the USA
Middletown, DE
15 September 2015